Dear Parent:

Congratulations! Your child is taking the first steps on an exciting journey. The destination? Independent reading!

STEP INTO READING® will help your child get there. The program offers five steps to reading success. Each step includes fun stories and colorful art. There are also Step into Reading Sticker Books, Step into Reading Math Readers, Step into Reading Phonics Readers, Step into Reading Write-In Readers, and Step into Reading Phonics Boxed Sets—a complete literacy program with something to interest every child.

Learning to Read, Step by Step!

Ready to Read   Preschool–Kindergarten
• big type and easy words • rhyme and rhythm • picture clues
For children who know the alphabet and are eager to begin reading.

Reading with Help   Preschool–Grade 1
• basic vocabulary • short sentences • simple stories
For children who recognize familiar words and sound out new words with help.

Reading on Your Own   Grades 1–3
• engaging characters • easy-to-follow plots • popular topics
For children who are ready to read on their own.

Reading Paragraphs   Grades 2–3
• challenging vocabulary • short paragraphs • exciting stories
For newly independent readers who read simple sentences with confidence.

Ready for Chapters   Grades 2–4
• chapters • longer paragraphs • full-color art
For children who want to take the plunge into chapter books but still like colorful pictures.

STEP INTO READING® is designed to give every child a successful reading experience. The grade levels are only guides. Children can progress through the steps at their own speed, developing confidence in their reading, no matter what their grade.

Remember, a lifetime love of reading starts with a single step!

For Ray Arps
—M.L.

Published in the United States by Random House Children's Books, a division of Random House,
Inc., 1745 Broadway, New York, NY 10019, and in Canada by Random House of Canada Limited,
Toronto, in conjunction with Disney Enterprises, Inc.

Step into Reading, Random House, and the Random House colophon are registered trademarks of
Random House, Inc.

Visit us on the Web!
www.stepintoreading.com
www.randomhouse.com/kids
Educators and librarians, for a variety of teaching tools, visit us at
www.randomhouse.com/teachers

Library of Congress Cataloging-in-Publication Data
Lagonegro, Melissa.
The spooky sound / by Melissa Lagonegro ; illustrated by Ron Cohee.
p. cm. — (Step into reading. Step 2 book)
ISBN 978-0-7364-2664-0 (trade) — ISBN 978-0-7364-8079-6 (lib. bdg.)
I. Cohee, Ron. II. Cars (Motion picture) III. Title.
PZ7.L14317Sp 2010 [E]—dc22 2009023863

Printed in the United States of America   10 9 8 7 6 5

DISNEY · PIXAR

Cars

The Spooky Sound

By Melissa Lagonegro
Illustrated by Ron Cohee

Random House 🏠 New York

Lightning McQueen
and Mater like to tell
spooky stories.

Their friends are scared!
But Mater and Lightning
are not.

Lightning and Mater
drive home.
Ahhhoo!
They hear
a spooky sound.

They want
to find out
what it is.

Lightning and
Mater drive by
Ramone's paint shop.
Ahhhoo!

Mater sees
a scary shape.
Is it a monster?

Lightning goes
into the shop.
He finds paint cans!
He tells Mater
there is no monster.

They drive
by Doc's shop.
It is open late.
Ahhhoo!

The sound is louder.
They see
sparks and flames.
Is it a fire monster?

Mater is scared.

But there is

no fire monster.

Doc is fixing Sarge.

The cars drive
to Casa Della Tires.
Ahhhoo!
The sound is closer.
Mater sees
a creepy shape.

Is it a monster
with two heads?

Lightning finds
tall piles of tires.
Luigi and Guido
are having a sale.

Mater and Lightning
drive into the desert.
<u>Ahhhoo!</u>

Mater sees a light
in the sky.
Is it a monster
that glows?

Lightning spots
Al Oft.
He is taking
a night flight.

Lightning and Mater
keep driving.

Ahhhoo!

The sound is right

behind them!

Mater is really scared!

Lightning wants
to find the sound.
He turns around
very slowly.

The spooky sound
is not a monster!
It does not have fire.
It does not have
two heads.

It does not glow.

It is Sheriff!

He is driving

in his sleep!

Lightning and Mater
laugh and laugh.
They are
not afraid!

But then they see
two glowing eyes!
Oh, no!
What is it?

They do not want
to find out!